ROMPING MONSTERS, STOMPING MONSTERS

JANE YOLEN

illustrated by KELLY MURPHY

WALKER BOOKS
AND SUBSIDIARIES
LONDON • BOSTON • SYDNEY • AUCKLAND

First published 2013 by Walker Books Ltd
87 Vauxhall Walk, London SE11 5HJ

2 4 6 8 10 9 7 5 3 1

This book has been typeset in Wilke Bold

Printed in China

British Library Cataloguing in Publication Data:
a catalogue record for this book is available from the British Library

ISBN 978-1-4063-4386-1

www.walker.co.uk

For Ella and Anna MacLachlan,
who borrowed my house in the summer of 2012.
Hope you found enough books.
Here's one more.
J. Y.

For Antoine and his monsterly advice
K. M.

Monsters stretch.
Monsters twirl.

COURTS

Monsters catch.

Monsters hurl.

Monsters tumble,
Run and lope.

Monsters jump
A monster rope.

Monsters hopscotch.

Monsters slide.

Monsters swing
And piggy-back ride.

Monsters in
Three-legged races

Fall upon
Their monster faces.

Monsters teeter.

Monsters totter,

Monster faces
Red and hotter.

Monsters tickle,
Laugh – so jolly!

Monsters eat
A monster lolly.

Slurp
SLOP

Want a drink.

GULP
Grrrr

Grumble

GROWL

Say you're sorry.

All better now.